THE
GOLEM
OF
PRAGUE

Original title: *Frantz e il Golem*
© 2016, orecchio acerbo, Roma
www.orecchioacerbo.com
This translation published by arrangement with Anna Spadolini Agency, Milano
English text © 2017 Annick Press
English translation by Brigitte Waisberg
English edition edited by Chandra Wohleber
English edition designed by Kong Njo

Annick Press Ltd.

We acknowledge the support of the Canada Council for the Arts and the Ontario Arts Council, and the participation of the Government of Canada/la participation du gouvernement du Canada for our publishing activities.

Cataloging in Publication

Cohen-Janca, Irène, 1954–
[Frantz e il Golem. English]
        The Golem of Prague / Irène Cohen-Janca ; Maurizio A. C. Quarello, illustrator; Brigitte Waisberg, translator.

Issued in print and electronic formats.
Originally published in Italian under title: *Frantz e il Golem.*
Translated from the French edition: *Frantz et le Golem*
ISBN 978-1-55451-888-3 (hardcover).–ISBN 978-1-55451-890-6 (pdf).–
ISBN 978-1-55451-889-0 (epub)

        I. Quarello, Maurizio A. C., illustrator II. Waisberg, Brigitte, translator
III. Title. IV. Title: Frantz e il Golem. English.

PZ7.C665Go 2017   j853'.92   C2016-905511-6
                                                          C2016-905512-4

Published in the U.S.A. by Annick Press (U.S.) Ltd.
Distributed in Canada by University of Toronto Press.
Distributed in the U.S.A. by Publishers Group West.

Printed in China

Visit us at: www.annickpress.com

Also available in e-book format. Please visit www.annickpress.com/ebooks.html for more details. Or scan

THE GOLEM OF PRAGUE

STORY BY **IRÈNE COHEN-JANCA**

ART BY **MAURIZIO A.C. QUARELLO**

TRANSLATED BY BRIGITTE WAISBERG

January 21, 1892: Nighttime in Prague

Prague is fast asleep. The blue sky has grown dark. Everyone has gone inside. The lights have dimmed. Time stands still as a deep silence overtakes the city.

The moon opens one eye and peers through the windows.

In Rooster Lane, the old houses with their colorless walls and locked gates hug one another tightly as if to keep from falling down.

On the second floor of the last house, an oil lamp burns. It shines on a man with a black skullcap perched on his white hair. Aaron Wassertrum, the old puppeteer, is bent over a wooden table. He is making dolls, designing sets, and inventing magical stories to bring them to life.

While sewing a tiny velvet ribbon around the neck of a princess with blond hair and a purple robe, he mutters, "Oh, my wooden creatures, how I love making you come alive!"

On the third floor, the moon with its pearly brush touches the face of Miriam, daughter of Anschel Ginzburg, the junk dealer. Her porcelain complexion and delicate skin seem to be the very source of the moon's glow. She is fast asleep, breathing gently.

On the top floor, the silvery light lands on a small, empty room. The bed, which has not been slept in, belongs to Frantz Munka, son of the jeweler. Frantz said that tonight he would stay with his best friend, David Meshullan.

But where is Frantz really?

Earlier that Evening

Before night fell, Frantz crept out of Rooster Lane. But he did not go to David's house. Like a shadow gliding silently through Prague's laneways, he went in the opposite direction, toward Cervena Street and the Old New Synagogue.

A beggarwoman with a gray, wrinkled face cried out as he passed, "Where are you running like that, my boy? To an appointment with the devil?"

Frantz did not reply. He stopped only once along the way. He couldn't resist the sight of the old puppeteer standing in the square.

Whenever Aaron Wassertrum set up his puppet theater, children came running from every corner, their eyes gleaming with excitement.

A Lost Heart

On the stage draped in a red curtain and lit by flickering torches, the puppeteer was telling the story of two children who swore to love each other forever. A painted backdrop showed a beautiful garden with a large pool, an old stone staircase, and a moss-covered statue.

The children were exchanging their vows at the edge of the pool. The girl wanted to seal her pledge with the crimson heart strung around her neck on a black velvet ribbon. But as she handed it to the boy, the ribbon tore.

The heart rolled away and the boy was filled with despair. He searched for the heart while softly singing:

Where did the red stone heart go
That fell from your neck white as snow?
Where did the blood-red stone fall
That sealed our love once and for all?

Behind him, Punch, in his multicolored costume, was making faces. Everyone could hear his cruel laughter as he waved the ruby-red heart back and forth above his head. The children in the audience cried out, "It's there! It's there! Punch stole the heart."

Among the children, Frantz recognized Miriam. They hardly ever spoke when they ran into each other on the stairs or in the courtyard, but when they did, their words left a deep impression. Miriam wasn't shouting like the other children. She was staring wide-eyed at the scarlet heart dangling from Punch's fingers. In the dim light, her pale, translucent face shone like a piece of the moon. Frantz thought of the precious moonstone on his father's workbench, how it gave off a bluish-white light.

Suddenly, Miriam felt Frantz's presence. She turned toward him and stared, as if she was still watching the puppet show.

In the dying light, Miriam seemed unreal, dreamlike. Like the boy in the puppet show, Frantz was determined to find the heart. He ran as fast as he could.

Last Spring: The Forbidden Attic

As he ran, he remembered that day in the spring when the caretaker at the Old New Synagogue told the story of the Golem. In a solemn voice, he had begun to speak: "Long ago, in the Middle Ages, the Jews of Prague were under constant fear of death or expulsion. Rabbi Yehuda Loew, also known as the Maharal of Prague, was famous for his knowledge, wisdom, and courage. He decided to create a Golem, a giant made of clay, to protect the Jews of Prague. Nothing could vanquish or destroy it. But later, the Maharal smashed it to pieces. Its dusty remains were put in the attic of the Old New Synagogue."

He stopped talking and looked each boy in the eye before adding in a somber voice, "You must never try to go into the attic. Do not even open the trapdoor to look inside. One boy who tried went mad and another lost his life. Do you understand?"

A chorus of voices shouted Yes! so loudly the walls shook. Only Frantz Munka remained silent.

From then on, he never had a moment's peace. All he wanted was to enter the forbidden attic. He didn't dare mention it to anybody, not even his best friend, David. Frantz knew that David would refuse to take part in his insane plan and would tell on him for fear of seeing him die or go mad.

Torn between a gnawing curiosity and fear, he never let a day go by without passing by the Old New Synagogue or the ancient Jewish cemetery, close to the Vltava River.

On prayer days, he stood with his father under the vaulted stone ceiling of the synagogue, which now seemed alive and mysterious.

In the old cemetery, he contemplated the imposing tomb of the Maharal, which looked like a real building with its columns, carved garlands of fruit, and, on top, the symbol of the Maharal: a lion.

Today, January 21, 1892, Frantz decided to disobey the old caretaker. When he arrived at the corner of Maiselova Street, he looked up at the clock on the town hall. He loved this old clock with its two faces. They both said seven o'clock: the number seven on one and on the other, the letter zayin, the seventh letter in the Hebrew alphabet.

The little doorway on the north side of the synagogue was always open. Frantz looked around, then as quietly and as nimbly as a cat, he slipped through the half-open door. Whenever he had been in the synagogue before, it was like a beehive with the constant buzz of people praying, singing, and chattering. But now there was a deep silence that made him nervous.

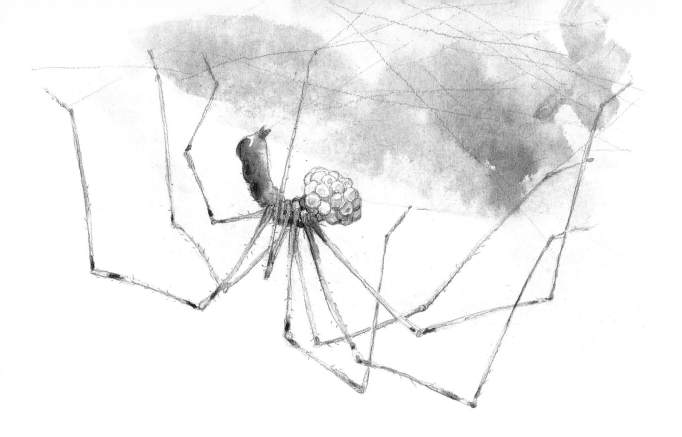

People said that at night the dead met there to study and pray. But they also said that angels had built the synagogue with stones taken from the ruins of Solomon's Temple in Jerusalem. And when a terrible fire almost destroyed the Jewish Quarter, two mysterious doves landed on the facade of the synagogue and, by beating their wings, they prevented the fire from spreading. Were they not the angels who always kept watch over the synagogue? Frantz felt somewhat reassured.

But as he climbed the stairway leading to the trapdoor to the attic, all his courage abandoned him. He shook so hard that he could barely move one foot in front of the other.

But it was too late to turn back. Terrified, he pushed the trapdoor to the attic open and went in.

There he found a small room with empty walls bathed in a pale light. Spiderwebs hung from the beams. Strewn across the dusty floor were old, torn prayer shawls, a cracked ram's horn, tarnished bronze candlesticks, and books, lots of yellowed books, stained with the bodies of dead flies. The moonlight made the cracks in the walls turn into grimacing figures and strange hieroglyphics. An indefinable and disturbing presence hung in the air.

Numbed by cold and fear, Frantz took shelter in a corner of the room. A beam of light crept across the floor, landing on a pile of old clothes. Shivering and feverish, he got up and went toward them. With fingers blue from the cold, and with a look of disgust, he picked up a huge, filthy gray coat covered in dust. He barely noticed the clumps of brownish dried mud all over it.

He put on the shabby coat, which looked like something straight out of the Middle Ages. And as he did so, everything started to sway.

Frantz felt the ground give way under his feet. His heart slowed and all his strength left him. He became more and more dizzy until he tripped and fell into the dust. He felt a pair of invisible hands grip his body and lift him up.

"It's surely the cold that has made me go numb, paralyzed me . . .," he said to himself as he sank into a deep sleep. He clenched his fists against the invisible powers transporting him, but a magnetic force swallowed him up, and, like a dry, dead leaf, he tumbled down into the bottom of a pit. In the bewitching light of the moon, eyes closed and fists clenched, Frantz crossed forbidden borders.

About Three Hundred Years Ago:
On the Other Side of Time

One dark winter's night in 1580, a man bent under the weight of a heavy load, entered the Jewish Quarter of Prague. He looked furtively over his shoulder, then stopped in front of the house of Shmuel the merchant. He crouched down and slid a bag through the basement window.

A few hours later, soldiers knocked violently at the door. "Are you Shmuel the Jew?"

"Yes, why?" asked Shmuel calmly. He had done nothing wrong.

"You have been denounced. We found the body of a child in your basement."

The soldiers threw themselves on him, tied his wrists, and carried him off to prison.

This kind of thing happened time and time again. The enemies of the Jews wanted people to believe that they drank the blood of Christians. The Jews tried to defend themselves, saying that their faith prohibited even tasting the blood of animals.

But the Angel of Death had already spread its wings over the old Jewish Quarter of Prague. Cries and prayers rang out in the synagogues; houses filled with the sound of sobbing and sighing. Shmuel had been sentenced to death. Hatred had awoken a volcano whose fiery lava threatened to destroy all the Jews in the Old Town. What was there to do but pray, shed tears, and hope for better times?

One man refused to bow down before such injustice and cruelty: Rabbi Loew, the Maharal of Prague. Everyone admired him, even the emperor, Rudolf II, who respected his intellect and his knowledge of philosophy, mathematics, and astronomy. He also stood in awe of the Maharal's superior grasp of the Kabbalah, the study of Jewish mysticism.

It is time for the persecution to stop, decided the Maharal of Prague. He asked the powers above, "How shall we battle evil?" The answer came in a dream:

MAKE A GOLEM OUT OF CLAY.

The Maharal understood the value of letters and the power of their combinations to form words. He studied the sacred texts looking for paths to wisdom, and examined all the letters of the Hebrew alphabet to discover their secrets.

The Maharal of Prague decided to make a Golem using those sacred letters and clay from the land. He summoned his two most loyal disciples, Yitzhak and Jacob, saying to them, "I am going to make a Golem, and I need your help because in order to create it, four elements are required: fire, water, air, and earth. You, Yitzhak, are the fire, and, Jacob, you are the water. I will be the air. The three of us will create the Golem from the fourth element, the earth.

The Maharal stood tall before them in his enormous velvet cloak, with his majestic mane of white hair. Under his fiery glance, his terrified disciples stood frozen.

The Maharal said to them, "What are you afraid of? Are you frightened by the mystery of the Golem? Isn't a child born out of love even more mysterious? We are simply talking about creating a body without a soul. Go, study and pray and come back when I call you."

At midnight the next day, the three men left the Old Town. In the darkness, they made their way to the Vltava. There, on the riverbank, the Maharal stopped, raised his staff, and pointed to a specific spot. By torchlight, the disciples silently dug up clay and piled it high, forming a human body twelve feet tall.

At dawn, the massive body lay unmoving in front of them, its face turned to the sky. The Maharal said to Yitzhak, "You are the fire. Walk around the body seven times from right to left while reciting the glorious names of God." The clay body began to dry, then gave off heat before taking on the blazing color of fire.

The Maharal turned to Jacob and said, "You are the water. Walk around the body seven times from left to right while pronouncing the sacred names of God."

The fire went out and water flowed through the clay body, making hair, toenails, and fingernails grow.

The Maharal drew strange, slanted eyes and a nose on its face, but no mouth.

"You will be like us, although stronger, but you will not have the gift of language because you do not have a soul."

He walked around the body, then traced three Hebrew letters on its forehead:

Tav   Mem   Aleph

Trembling, the disciples made out the word *Emet*. They knew that *Emet* means "truth." They also knew that if you remove the first letter, aleph, the word that is left is *Met*. "Dead."

The three men dressed the body in a huge, gray coat. Then they bowed down in front of it and said together, "And he breathed life into him and the man became a living creature."

The Golem let out a long sigh, then opened his eyes and looked around in amazement.

The Maharal pointed to him and commanded, "Get up! Your mission on earth is to protect the Jews!"

Slowly, the clay giant stood up, tall like a mountain.

Yitzhak and Jacob, frozen in fear and admiration, cried out, "Golem! Golem!"

There were already rumblings from the old Jewish Quarter. The hangman of Prague was putting up the gallows for Shmuel the merchant. The hate-filled crowd was rushing toward the city gates.

"Quick! Let us go!" ordered the Maharal.

Yitzhak and Jacob were stunned to see the giant move effortlessly, as if he were floating in the air. His feet barely touched the ground.

When they reached the gate at the entrance to the Old Town, they found that the guards had deserted the watchtowers. Men on foot or on horseback, armed with spears, axes, scythes, and nail-studded clubs, were trying to break down the gate. Women were screaming and children were throwing stones.

Again, the Maharal pointed to the Golem and gave a command, "Fulfill your mission: protect the Jews of Prague."

The Golem took a step forward. His head reached up to the second-story windows. His body was as large as the houses. Calmly, he moved through the frenzied crowd. He lifted up men and beasts as if they were wisps of straw and used his fists to destroy anything that blocked his way. Paralyzed with fear, some people did not try to run away but closed their eyes, waiting for death. Others ran as fast as they could. All around him, men and animals rushed around like insects. The Golem flattened them with his hand. Some people tried to fight him, but the arrows launched at the Golem slid down his body like thin rivulets of water. Spears barely pierced the clay before falling to the ground. Soon, the terrified attackers drew back, realizing they could neither kill nor wound the Golem. He was indestructible.

The Golem turned and walked toward the Maharal, who had not budged. With his eyes cast down, he was waiting for the creature. Together, they went through the Paryska Gate while, one after another, the Jews came out of their homes through the barricaded windows and doors.

A long and joyful cry arose, "Golem! Golem!"

But the Golem's face showed no emotion; he had a strange look that made those who came near him uneasy.

Time passed and the Jews of Prague now lived in peace. It was not only the Golem's superhuman strength that protected them; he also knew how to uncover and foil plots. He wandered in the cemeteries looking for open tombs from which children's bodies had been taken. They were going to be used to frame the Jews. He explored secret cellars and apartments where people were conspiring. He could see what was hidden and what would happen. He could look into people's hearts, hear their secret thoughts, and understand the language of animals and the earth.

Eva, the Maharal's learned and beloved daughter, asked, "How can the Golem see the future?"

"In the Talmud, Adam is called Golem, which means 'body without a soul.' During the first twelve hours of his existence, that's what he was, and he was able to see into the future. But once he became a complete man, with a soul, he lost that power. Only this unfinished creature still has it."

"So the Golem will never become a real man?"

"No, Eva, never. He will never have the divine spark that gives us a soul and the power of speech. But he *can* see the future."

Every time the Maharal sent him on a mission, the Golem came back victorious. He followed the Maharal so faithfully that sometimes their two shadows seemed to merge to make a single enormous one that stood out against the Prague sky.

At times, the Golem did not use his supernatural powers wisely. One day, the Maharal's wife asked the Golem to go and fetch some water to fill two large basins. The Golem took the pole with two buckets, went to the fountain, and, several hours later, the entire house was flooded. He did not understand that once the basins were filled, he had to stop.

More and more often, the Golem had nothing to do. He spent entire days motionless in a corner of the synagogue. In the Golem's troubled, veiled eyes, the Maharal thought he could see questions, "What is the secret behind my birth? What is the mystery behind my existence? Why am I not like other men? Now that my mission on earth is complete, am I of no use?"

When the Maharal gave him an order, the Golem no longer responded right away, and in his eerie eyes, the Maharal sensed a hint of defiance.

Then one terrible day, the Golem staggered out of the synagogue in a blind rage, his arms thrown up to the sky. He ran down to the Old Town and made his way to the riverbank, destroying everything in his path. Gripped by panic, the people ran, shouting, "Help! The Golem has gone mad! The Golem has gone mad!"

But no one could stop him or calm him down.

"Where is the Maharal? We can't find him anywhere."

Suddenly, in the middle of the road where the Golem was on his rampage, appeared Miriam, a young girl whose face was so pale that it looked like a moonstone. The Golem stopped in his tracks and knelt in front of her. All his anger evaporated and his eyes shone with joy. Miriam did not move. Fearlessly, she smiled at the Golem. The Golem brought his strange mouthless face, with its waxy complexion and slanted eyes, close to hers.

At that moment, Miriam saw a huge man coming toward her. His hair and long beard were white. He wore a fur hat and was wrapped in a large velvet coat, which made him look as if he were surrounded by waves.

Turning to the Golem, he said, "Golem, you have fulfilled your destiny. You have saved countless lives. It is time for you to rest."

But the Golem did not hear a thing and continued to stare in wonder at Miriam's face.

The Maharal's hand, with its long, thin fingers, emerged from the wide sleeve of his coat. He pointed to Miriam. His voice and eyes filled with sadness, he ordered, "Child, erase the aleph."

The Golem kept on looking at the little girl with the moon-colored face. He stared at her with the pleasure and wonder of babies discovering the world.

Miriam raised her hand toward his forehead, and, with a simple gesture, she erased the letter aleph. What remained was the word *Met*. "Dead." Immediately, the Golem collapsed. A word had given him life and now a missing letter brought him death.

1892: Back in the Forbidden Attic

At that exact same moment, in the attic of the Old New Synagogue, Frantz emerged from his deep sleep. Shudders ran through his body; he felt as if he were being catapulted through the air by a strange force. He opened his eyes and looked around in dismay.

"Where am I?" he asked.

Little by little, he recognized the old attic, where several hours earlier he had tripped and fallen. How many hours, days, or years had passed? He tried to remember but could not.

Quick! He had to get out of there! He stood up, took off the huge coat that weighed heavily on him, and rushed out of the attic. As he was leaving, he looked up at the clock on the town hall. Five o'clock said the face with the numbers. Seven o'clock, zayin, said the face with the Hebrew letters. Frightened by this new mystery, Frantz did not even try to figure it out. As the sun was beginning to rise, he ran through the narrow, deserted streets of the Old Town.

January 22, 1892: A New Day

That entire day, Frantz walked around as if he were in a dream. He knew that he had crossed over into a strange land, but everything he had experienced there seemed real and out of reach at the same time. It was like having a tiny locked room in his head, a room without doors or windows where no one, not even he, could enter.

As he passed in front of the shop belonging to Anschel the junk dealer, he saw Miriam alone inside. He pushed open the creaking door. From floor to ceiling were piled-up old, rusted, broken tools. Frantz walked along the twisted, uneven floors, stepping over strange objects: shattered dishes, old rags, and newspapers. Standing there, Miriam looked like a rare and precious flower blooming in a dark, gloomy cave.

When Frantz reached her, she looked at him strangely, as if she had seen a ghost. She had dark circles under her eyes and was even paler than usual.

"Hello, Miriam. How are you?"

"All right, Frantz, but I did not sleep well last night."

"Did you have a bad dream?"

"No, I had a very strange dream."

Frantz was curious. "Tell me about it, Miriam."

She was silent.

"Miriam, we've never spoken about this, but when we grow up, we'll get married, won't we?"

"Yes, Frantz. I think we should get married in the future."

"So we should never keep secrets from each other. Tell me about your dream."

Miriam lowered her eyes and spoke softly, "I was walking in Prague, in our old neighborhood, but it wasn't really our neighborhood. I recognized the houses, the town hall, and even the clock with two faces, but it was another world. It wasn't our city. People were wearing strange clothes. I was walking along when, suddenly, a giant appeared close to the Old New Synagogue. He was in a rage. Everyone was running away from him. But when he saw me, he became calm. He knelt in front of me with a look of surprise and delight. At that moment, a very tall, old, majestic man, with a long white beard, surely a great rabbi, approached me and said, 'Child, erase the aleph.'

"I knew right away that I had to obey. I removed the aleph engraved on the giant's forehead."

Frantz thought he was losing his mind. His heart pounding, trembling in front of Miriam, who had so gently opened the locked little room inside him, he asked, "But, Miriam, weren't you afraid?"

"No."

"But how could you not have been afraid?"

"I don't dare tell you."

"You must, Miriam. We have made a vow to marry. Now we cannot keep secrets from each other."

Slowly, pronouncing each word carefully, Miriam answered, "I saw something in the giant's eyes that reminded me of you."

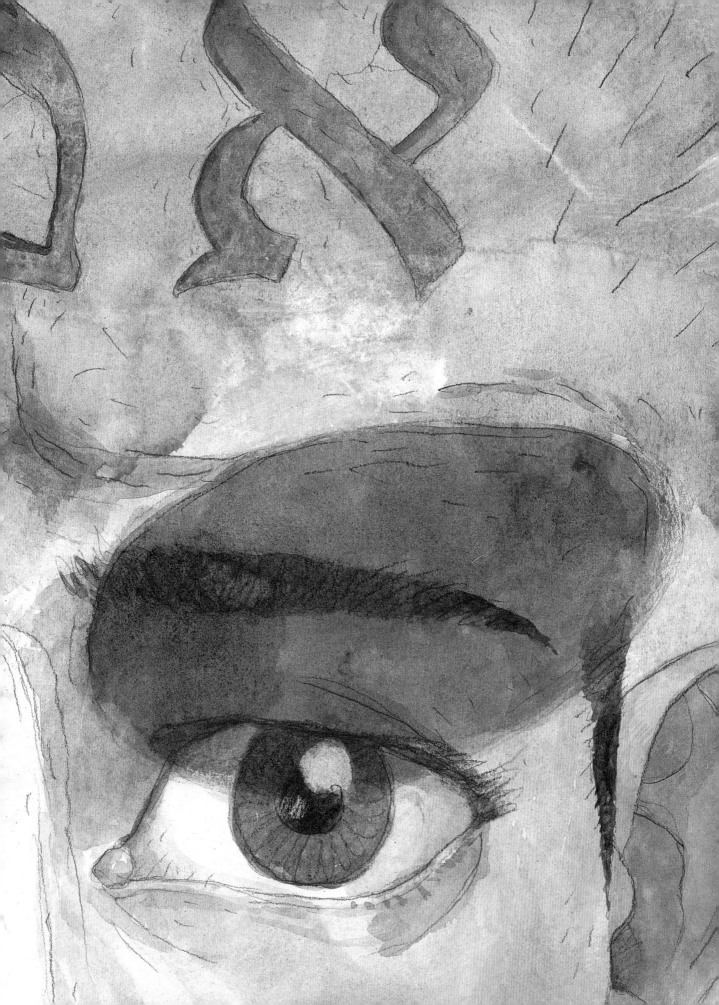

Glossary

Aleph Mem Tav

These three letters of the Hebrew alphabet are the equivalent of the letters *A*, *M*, and *T*. The first, aleph, can be pronounced like the "a" in "all" or like the "e" in "bed." Hebrew is written from right to left.

Golem

The story of the Golem is one of the oldest and most famous Jewish legends. Originally, the word *golem* referred to Adam before he was given a soul. It means "incomplete." In the sixteenth century, stories emerged of how the Golem came to be. He was described as a colossal creature made of clay and possessing supernatural powers.

Kabbalah

Kabbalah is the tradition of Jewish mysticism. Those who study Kabbalah believe that every word in the Bible explains the mystical origins of the universe.

Names of God

In the Old Testament, there are many different names for God, including *Adonai, Elohim*, and *El Shaddai*.

Rabbi Loew, the Maharal of Prague

Rabbi Loew ben Bezalel was a famous sixteenth-century biblical scholar and the chief rabbi of Prague. Highly respected for his knowledge, he was also known as a Jewish mystic and philosopher. He was commonly known as the Maharal of Prague. Maharal is the Hebrew acronym that stands for "Our Teacher, Rabbi Loew."

Synagogue

A synagogue is a Jewish house of prayer.

Talmud

The Talmud contains the teachings and writings of rabbis from the third to the seventh century of the Common Era. Their interpretations of what is written in the Bible form the basis of Jewish practices and traditions.

Zayin

Every letter in the Hebrew alphabet has a numerical value. Zayin is the seventh letter in the alphabet, so it can stand for the number seven.

About Irène Cohen-Janca

Irène was born in 1954 in Tunis, where she spent her childhood. After getting her university degree in modern literature, she became a librarian. Today, she lives in Essonne, France, where she is the collections manager at a public library. Irène has written many novels and picture books, including *Mister Doctor*, which has been translated into Korean, French, Spanish, German, and English from the original Italian.

About Maurizio A. C. Quarello

Maurizio was born in Turin, Italy, in 1974. There he studied graphic design, architecture, and illustration. After working in advertising and as a landscape artist, he decided to devote himself entirely to illustrating children's books. He has about 40 books to his name, many of which have received awards in France, Germany, Italy, Spain, Belgium, and Sweden. His work has been exhibited in galleries in over 15 countries. He now teaches illustration at the Academy of Fine Arts of Macerata (Italy).

By the Same Author and Illustrator

Nothing—not even the chance to live—makes Dr. Korczak abandon the children of the Warsaw Ghetto.

USBBY's Honor List of Outstanding International Books
Sydney Taylor Book Award, Notable Book
National Parenting Publications Award (NAPPA), Bronze
Independent Publishers Book Award, Gold

•

"Haunting and memorable."
—*Kirkus Reviews*, *starred review

"The remarkable true story of Dr. Janusz Korczak is told through
text and stunningly somber illustrations."
—*Literacy Daily*, International Reading Association

"This sensitively written history . . . belongs in all
Holocaust collections."
—Association of Jewish Libraries

"Emotionally evocative and haunting illustrations
enhance this beautiful book."
—*Jewish Book Council*, *starred review